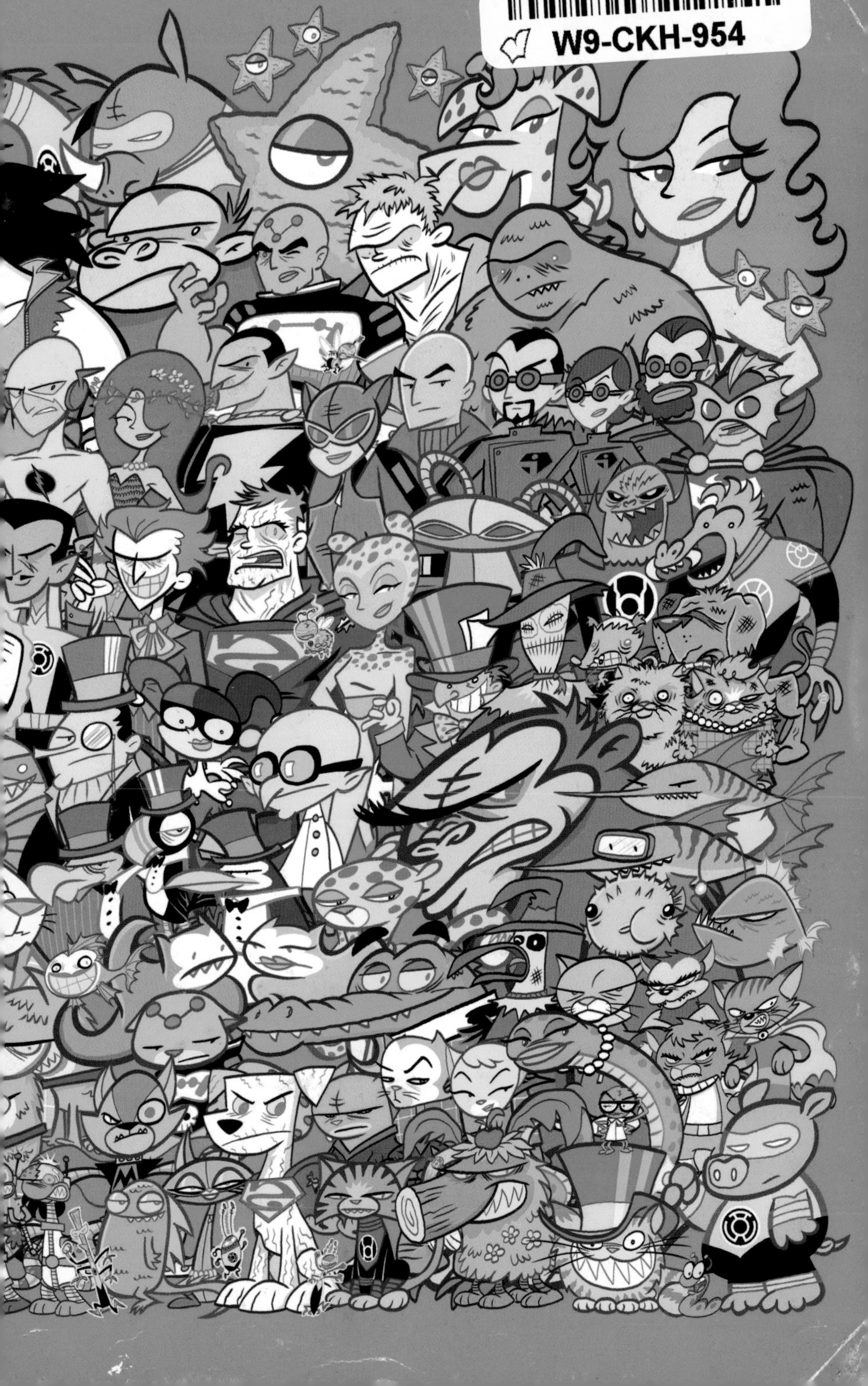

DC SUPER-PETS!

by John
Sazaklis

DEEP-SEA
DUEL

illustrated by
Art Baltazar

Aquaman created by Paul Norris

Picture Window Books™
a capstone imprint

Starring...

EVIL HENCH-FISH!

FLUFFY
THE GOLDFISH!

GEOFFREY!

BETTY!

OCEAN MASTER!

AQUALAD AND THE AQUA-FAMILY!

TABLE OF CONTENTS!

SUPER-PET HERO FILE 019:
AQUA-PETS

FLUFFY
Species: Goldfish
Power: Power Bowl
Favorite Food:
Fish Flakes

BETTY
Species: Beluga
Power: Whale Tail
Favorite Food:
Jumbo Shrimp

GEOFFREY
Species:
Hammerhead Shark
Power: Thick Skull
Favorite Food:
Crab Cakes

Super Hero Owner:
AQUALAD

Super Hero Owner:
NICOLETTA

Super Hero Owner:
MERA

Super-Pet Enemy File 019:
EVIL HENCH-FISH

JOEY
Species: Swordfish
Power: Needle Nose

JOHNNY
Species: Swordfish
Power: Sharp Snout

FRANKIE
Species: Anglerfish
Power: Bright Ideas

GEORGE
Species: Blowfish
Power: Swollen Head

Super-villain Owner:
OCEAN MASTER

Chapter 1

AQUA-FAMILY REUNION

In the underwater kingdom of Atlantis, **King Arthur** and his queen, **Mera**, got ready for a family reunion. The couple decorated the palace with beautiful coral. They covered long tables with mouth-watering meals.

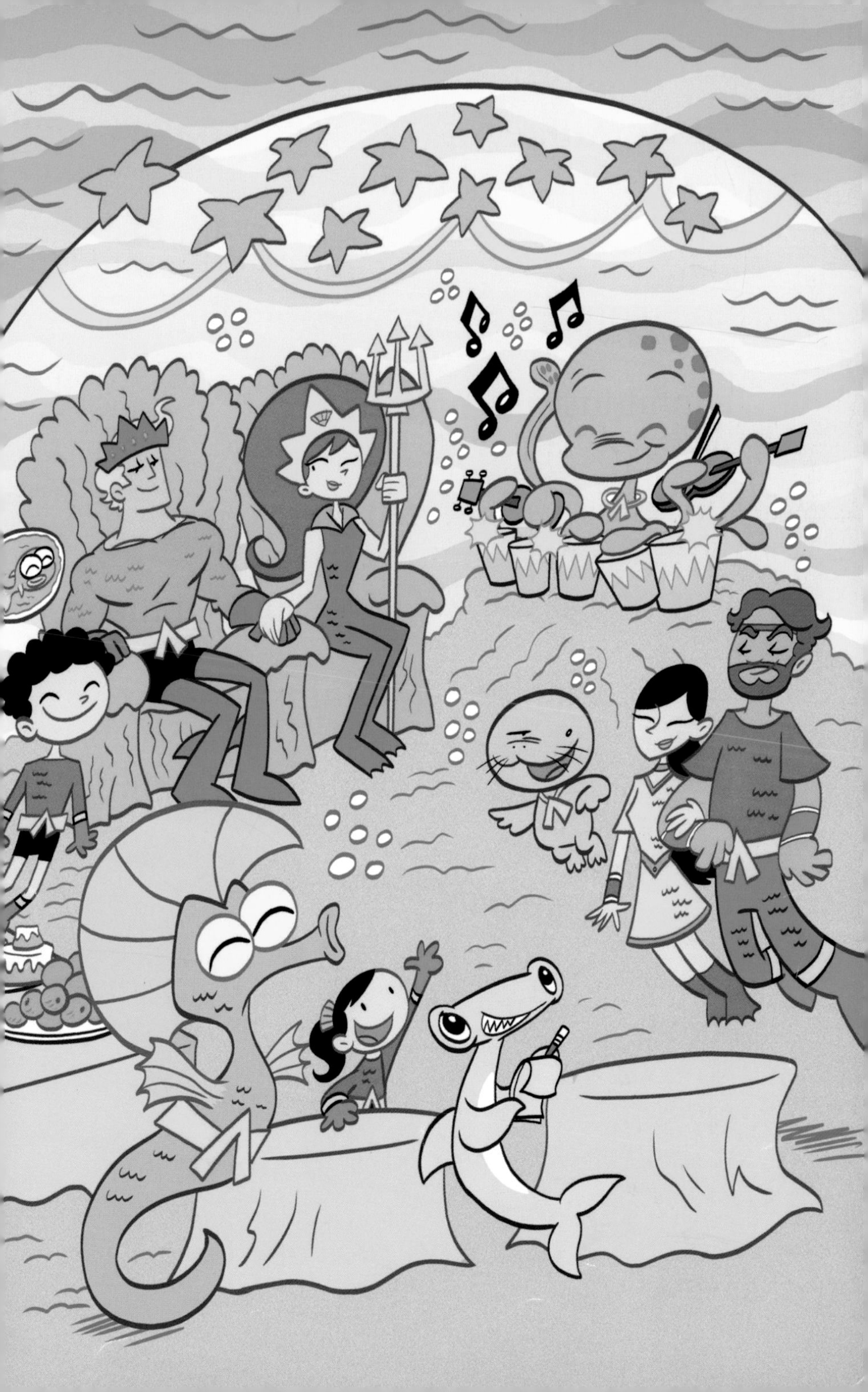

King Arthur, also known as the super hero **Aquaman**, spoke with his sea creatures. He gave them plenty of helpful tasks to perform.

Ark the seal greeted guests at the door. Storm the sea horse showed them to their seats. For entertainment, Topo the octopus played his ukulele, violin, and drums . . . all at once!

Even Mera's pet, **Geoffrey** the shark, enjoyed his role as a waiter. He swam up and down the aisles. He made sure each glass and plate was always full.

Family and friends from the
farthest reaches of the ocean came for
the festivities. Aquaman's sidekick,
Aqualad, was there. He even brought
along his aqua-pet, **Fluffy** the goldfish,
in a special freshwater bubble.

Mera's niece, **Nicoletta**, arrived with her pet as well. They had come from Poseidonis, the capital of Atlantis.

The young mermaid floated toward Aqualad. "Hi, I'm Nicoletta," she said. "And this is **Betty**, my baby beluga."

"I'm Aqualad," replied the junior hero. "But you can call me Garth." He shook Betty's fin and Nicoletta's hand.

"I know who you are," said Nicoletta with a smile. "I'm your biggest fan. I follow all of your adventures!"

Aqualad blushed. "Is there a warm current coming through, or is it just me?" A bubble bumped up against his back. "Oh, uh, this is my pet, Fluffy!"

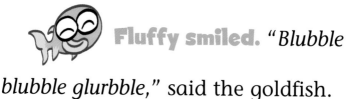 **Fluffy smiled.** "*Blubble blubble glurbble*," said the goldfish.

"Fluffy says 'It's nice to meet you,'" Aqualad said.

"Lovely. Now let's have some fun!" Nicoletta said, pulling Garth through the courtyard. Their pets followed close behind, swishing their tails to keep up.

Aqualad was excited to make a new friend. "I can show you around the palace, or we can go down to Blackbeard's Knoll," he said. "It's full of sunken pirate ships. **I hear it's haunted by a skeleton crew!"**

 "Ooh, that sounds scary," Nicoletta said. "Let's go!"

Before they could get far, the new friends bumped into the Sea King and Queen Mera. "And just where do you think you're going?" they asked.

"Aunt Mera!" Nicoletta cried out. "Garth was just showing me around the palace, that's all."

"They're going to the old shipyard!" squealed Betty. She started shivering at the thought of ghost pirates.

"Well, in that case," Mera began, crossing her arms, "Geoffrey is going with you." The queen whistled. A hammerhead shark swam to her side.

"Never you fear, my lady," Geoffrey said. "I shall protect these youngsters."

"I, too, was a scrappy troublemaker at your age," Aquaman admitted. The Sea King messed up Aqualad's hair. Then he clapped the young hero on the back. "Now off you go! Be safe . . . and be back before dessert!"

As the new friends swam off, a stranger floated in the shadows of a nearby cavern. He watched the party goers laugh, sing, and dance. He was boiling with anger.

The stranger held a powerful trident in his hand. With this weapon, he could shoot magical energy beams.

Suddenly, the trident started glowing. The water around the man bubbled from the heat.

FWOOSH! The mystery man jetted out of the darkness.

It was Orm Curry, Aquaman's half-brother, and the pirate super-villain known as **Ocean Master!**

"What kind of reunion doesn't include the *whole* family?" Orm asked two evil swordfish floating next to him.

"Maybe your invite got lost at sea," said the swordfish named Johnny.

"Or maybe they just forgot," added Joey, the other swordfish.

"A true ruler never forgets," said the villain. "Aquaman should make way for a new King of the Sea . . . ME!"

Two more evil hench-fish arrived at the villain's side. Frankie, an anglerfish, could shoot bolts of electricity from his forehead.

George the blowfish could poke his enemies with toxic spikes.

"The gang's all here," said Orm. "Our attack on Atlantis can begin!"

Ocean Master raised his trident. Then he placed one foot on each swordfish and charged toward the palace. **"Prepare for the fall of the House of Arthur!"**

UNDERWATER PLUNDER

Garth, Nicoletta, and their fishy friends arrived at Blackbeard's Knoll. Rows of sunken ships lined the ocean floor like tombstones in a graveyard.

"I don't think it's wise to be here," said Betty. The baby beluga shivered in the cold, dark water.

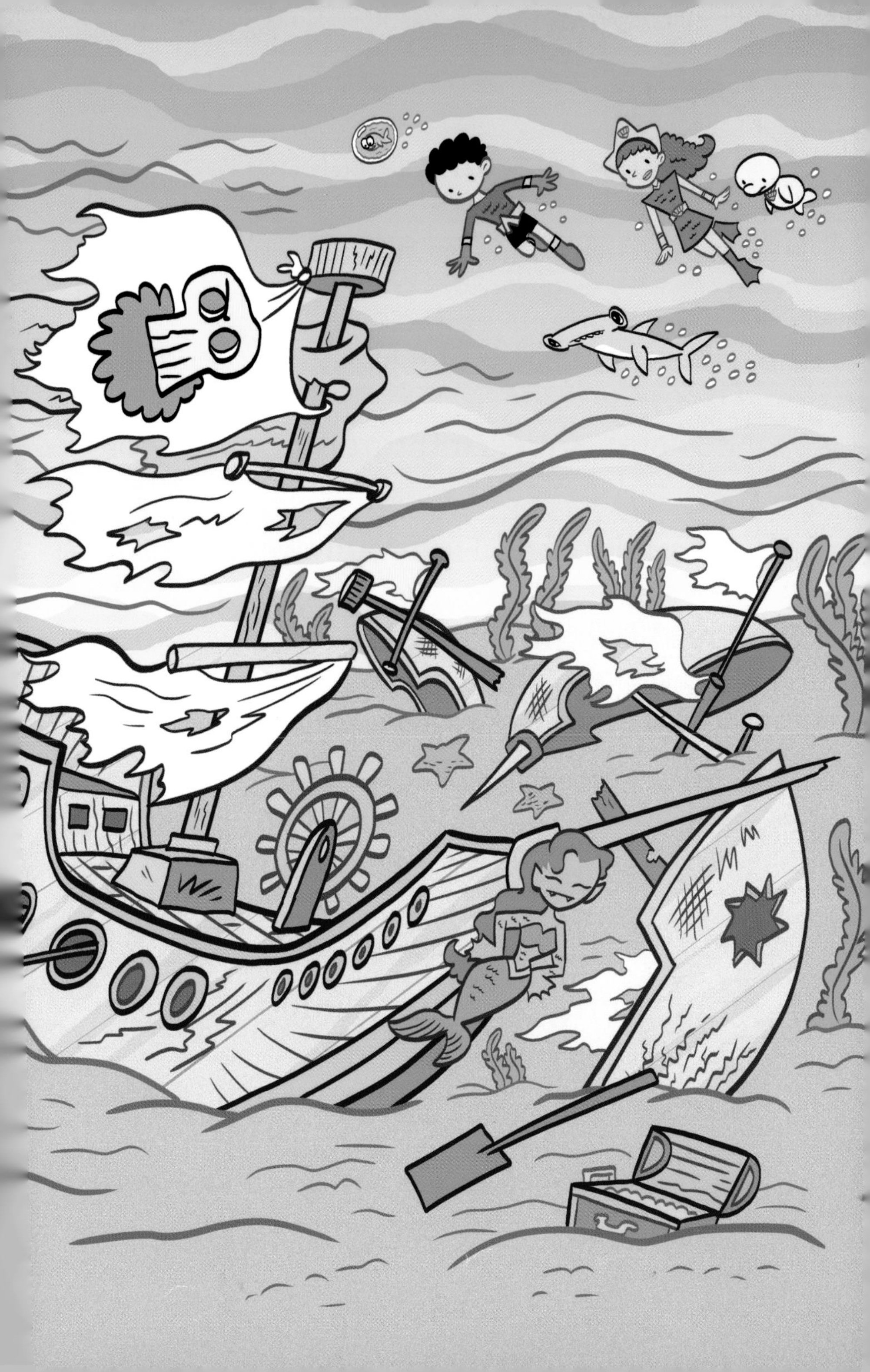

Garth, Fluffy, and Nicoletta swam closer to the largest sunken ship.

"This must be Blackbeard's," said Nicoletta, squeezing through a porthole.

Aqualad and Fluffy followed. Geoffrey stayed behind with Betty, who was too scared to go inside. "Don't worry," said Aqualad. "We'll be right back."

The three friends swam through the ship's galley. In an old dining cabin, they spotted a table covered in silver and gold. "Treasure!" Aqualad shouted.

Suddenly, the ship shifted in the water. The seat at the head of the table whirled around to face the trio. Sitting in the chair was an old pirate captain — or what was left of him.

"Great Guppies!" cried Aqualad. "It's the ghost of Blackbeard!"

The pirate ship shifted again. The skeleton jolted forward.

 "Ahhh!" screamed Nicoletta. **"Swim for your lives!"**

The terrified trio sped out of the porthole and away from the ship. Geoffrey and Betty swam after them.

 "So Captain Blackbeard doesn't like uninvited guests?" joked Geoffrey.

 "I think we'd better get back to Atlantis," Garth replied. "We'll be much safer there."

Meanwhile, at the kingdom, the party had moved from the courtyard to the grand ballroom. The ceiling above was a large glass dome looking up into a sea full of starfish. The Atlanteans all sang. They took turns dancing with their king and queen.

Suddenly, the room shook. The walls heated up, nearly boiling the water around them. Topo stopped playing music. The puzzled guests started asking questions.

"Something fishy is going on here,"
Aquaman said. He closed his eyes. The
hero used his mind powers to scan the
waves around the building. "Oh no!"
he cried.

The beautiful dome exploded in a
shower of glass and light. SMASH!
Ocean Master appeared through a
flurry of bubbles. His hench-fish circled
the water around him.

"I thought it best to arrive
fashionably late!" the villain said.

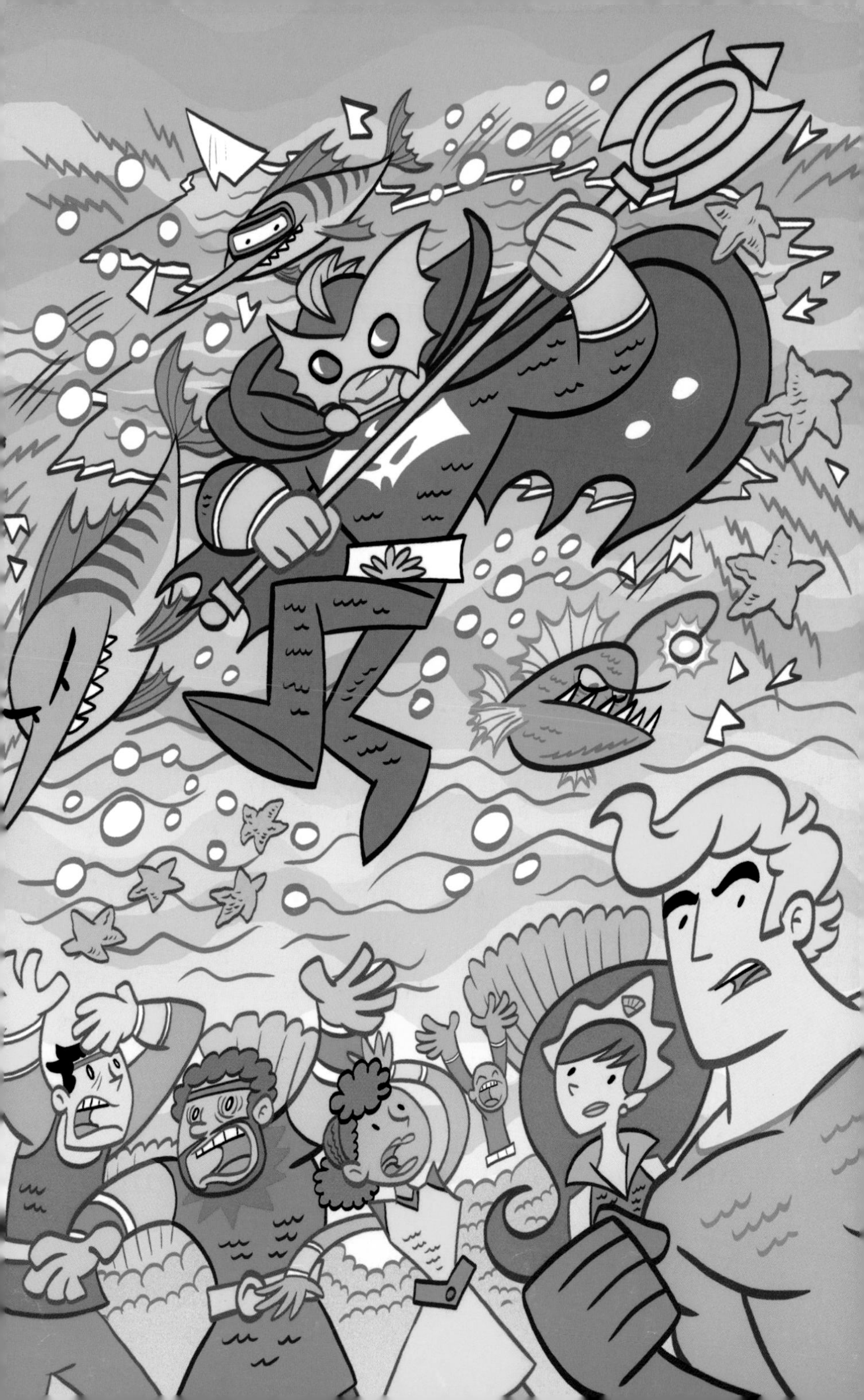

 **"You weren't invited, Orm,"** said the Sea King. "You're too crabby for this crowd." Aquaman moved in front of his guests, protecting them from the villain.

"What kind of king wears such a ridiculous outfit?" asked Orm. "The throne of Atlantis belongs to me!"

"Come and get it!" Aquaman said.

The brothers charged at each other. Storm, Topo, and Ark swam alongside Aquaman. They sped toward Ocean Master's hench-fish.

The villain held his trident over his head. The weapon glowed with electric energy. As the royal guards hurried to their leader's aid, the villain zapped them with his trident. ZZZAP!

They were frozen in place.

BOOOM! Ocean Master unleashed another powerful blast at Aquaman and Mera. The heroes were trapped in a shatterproof bubble.

"Atlantis and all its riches are mine now!" Ocean Master said.

Then the villain made himself

comfortable on the throne. At the

same time, Aquaman sent a telepathic

message to Aqualad that Atlantis

was in danger. The tiny titan was the

kingdom's only hope.

SEA SAVIOR

As the kids fled the shipyard, Garth stopped mid-swim. Something was wrong! **HUMMMM!** It was Aquaman's telepathic message.

"Atlantis is under attack by the Ocean Master!" Aqualad gasped.

 **"Suffering sea slugs!"** Betty the beluga cried. "I'd rather take my chances with Blackbeard's ghost."

"We must hurry!" said Geoffrey the shark. "Climb on my back."

Aqualad grabbed Fluffy's bubble and hopped on the hammerhead. Nicoletta and Betty joined them. As they sped back to the palace, Aqualad worried that it might be too late.

As the castle came into view, the friends saw the damage to the dome.

The friends and their pets moved
closer. Staying out of sight, they
peeked through the hole in the dome.
The group saw Ocean Master and his
crummy crew making a mess of the
throne room.

"Grrr!" Geoffrey the hammerhead growled. "Allow me to scrape that briny barnacle off the king's throne!"

Aqualad stopped the hotheaded hammerhead. "We need to work as a team for this royal rescue," said the young hero.

"Garth is right," Nicoletta said, smiling. "He's the professional here."

 "I'd like to point out that belugas are smarter than some humans," Betty said. "I can help with the plan."

Back in the throne room, the hench-fish, Frankie and George, carried a treasure chest to Ocean Master. Johnny and Joey used their pointy noses to pick the lock.

WHUMP! The chest popped open. A pile of Atlantean gold and precious stones sparkled in the light.

"Ah, such regal riches," said the pirate. "It's good to be the king!"

"You're not the king!" a voice echoed through the chamber. "You're just a royal pain!"

Ocean Master looked up to see

a small figure shadowed against

the broken dome. **"Well, if it isn't**

Aquaman Junior," he said.

"The name's Aqualad," said the tiny

titan. "And I'm here to put an end to

your rule."

Ocean Master laughed. Then he turned to his hench-fish. **"Turn this chump into chum,"** he commanded.

As the fishy foes torpedoed toward Aqualad, he swam aside to reveal the plan of attack. A seaweed slingshot!

Nicoletta and Betty had stretched out a long strand of seaweed. Nicoletta placed Fluffy's hard bubble in the middle. She pulled back until the seaweed was tight. As the scary sea creatures got closer, Nicoletta released Fluffy and let him fly. *FWOOSH!*

The aqua-pet pin-balled his way
through the enemies. First, he bonked
Johnny on the head. Then he bounced
off Joey. Then Frankie and George. The
dizzy hench-fish rubbed their heads
and then chased after Fluffy.

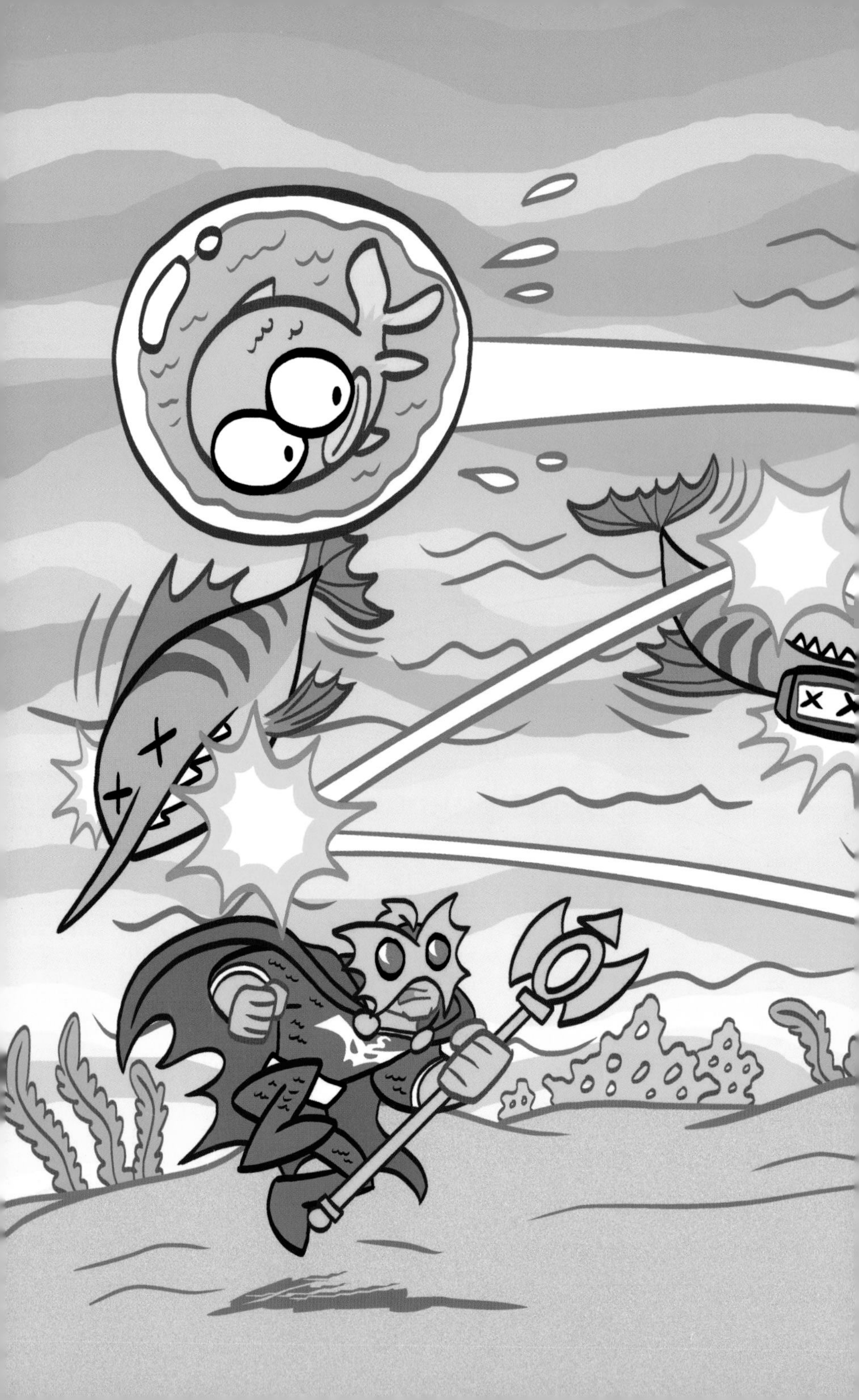

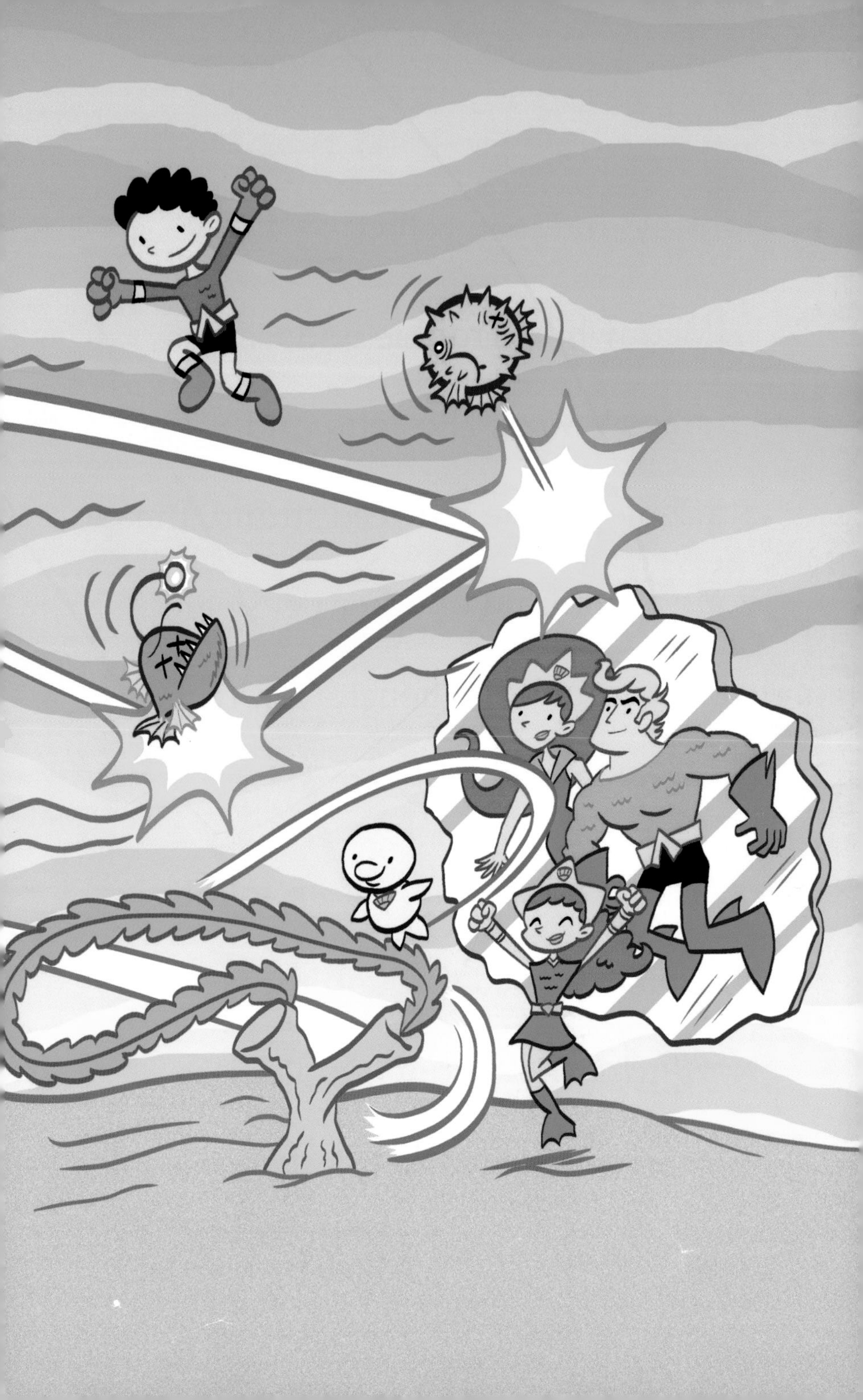

"We're gonna burst your bubble!"

Johnny and Joey yelled.

Meanwhile, Frankie and George charged toward Nicoletta and Betty. Still holding the seaweed strand, the young mermaid and her pet swam circles around the hench-fish, tying them together.

George puffed himself up to full size. His spikes ripped through the seaweed. Now he and the angry anglerfish were free. Frankie shot electric bolts at Nicoletta and Betty. **ZRRRRRT!!**

They dived behind a banquet table.
The bolts blasted off the silverware,
exploding in a shower of sparks.

Aqualad climbed onto Geoffrey's
back. They sped toward Ocean Master.
The villain pointed his trident at the
junior hero and fired an energy blast.

Geoffrey flipped backward over
the energy beam. The blast missed
its mark and hit Frankie and George
instead. They were knocked out and
floated belly-up toward the ceiling.

"Looks like that mean mackerel got a taste of his own medicine," Betty whispered to Nicoletta.

"Are you sure you know how to use that thing?" Aqualad asked as he leaped toward Ocean Master. He grabbed the trident.

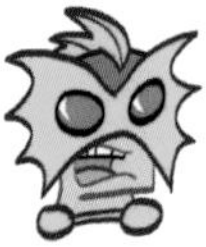

"How dare you!" Ocean Master yelled. He struggled with the tiny titan. Geoffrey came to Aqualad's aid. He head-butted Ocean Master in the belly.

POOOM! The impact separated the pirate from his weapon.

Aqualad grabbed the trident. The young hero held Ocean Master at bay.

"I don't need that trinket to handle you, Aqua-brat!" yelled the villain. He lunged at the young sidekick.

Suddenly, Fluffy came zooming between Aqualad and Ocean Master. Following close behind were Johnny and Joey. The goldfish pushed his owner out of the way. The silly swordfish couldn't control their speed. They slammed into Ocean Master.

WHUMP! Ocean Master was pinned to the throne by his swordfish. Their snouts had poked through his cape on either side.

"Blast you, Aqualad!" yelled the villain.

"Don't mind if I do," said the young hero. He fired the trident at his friends. The blast reversed the spell on the frozen kingdom. Atlantis was safe.

Aquaman thanked Aqualad, Fluffy, and their friends for saving the day.

Then, the Sea King swam to his half-brother. "Well, Orm, you wanted the throne of Atlantis. Now you're *stuck* with it!" Aquaman said.

"I believe he gets the *point*," Mera said. "Both of them."

The heroes all laughed. Then, the king ordered the party to continue. And, as a fair ruler, Aquaman allowed Ocean Master and his pets to be a part of the event. He even promised them a place to stay . . . in the palace prison!

END!

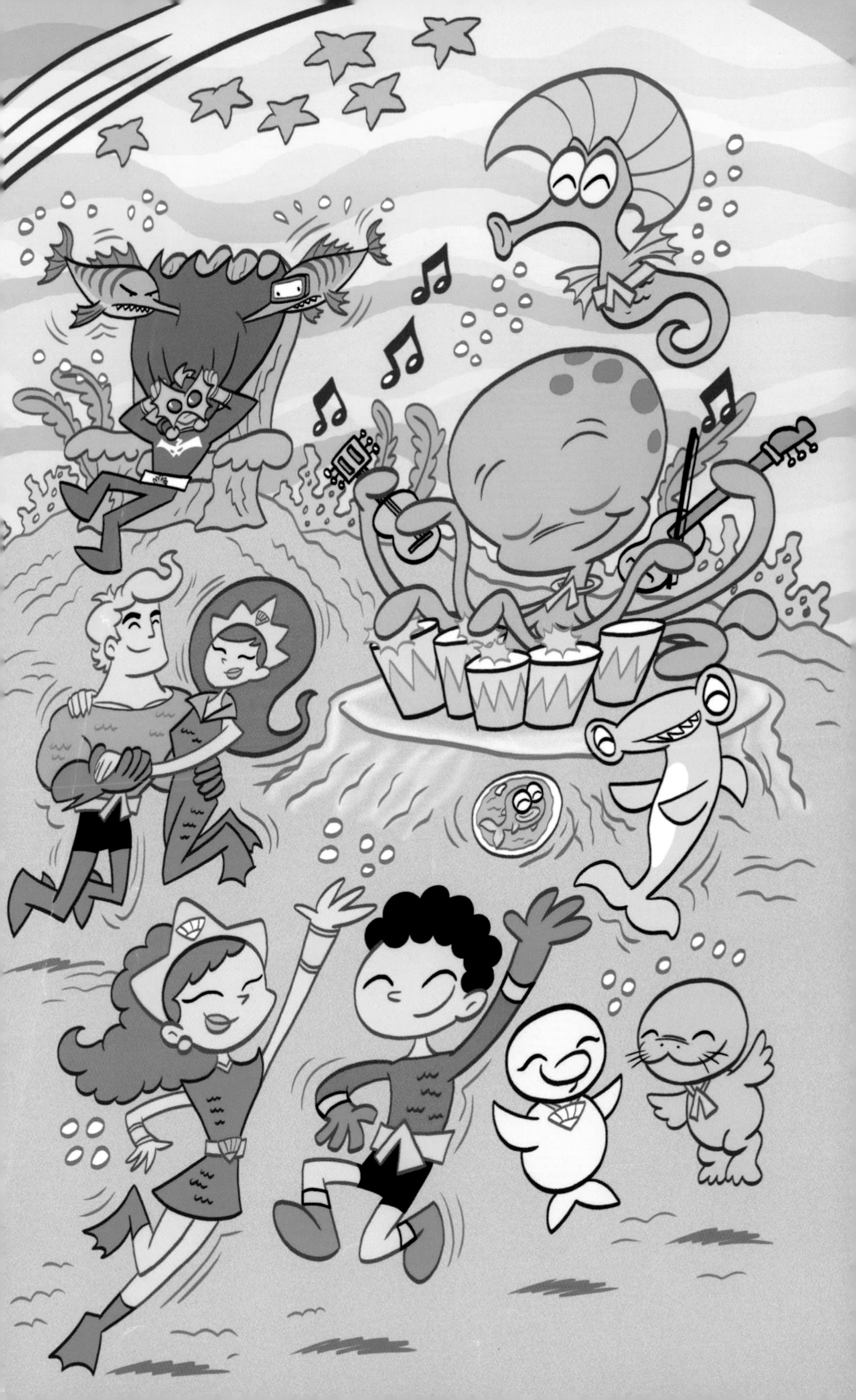

KNOW YOUR HERO PETS

1. Krypto
2. Streaky
3. Whizzy
4. Comet
5. Beppo
6. Super-Turtle
7. Fuzzy
8. Ace
9. Robin Robin
10. Batcow
11. Jumpa
12. Whatzit
13. Hoppy
14. Tawky Tawny
15. Spot
16. Plastic Frog
17. Gleek
18. Big Ted
19. Dawg
20. Space Dolphins
21. Proty
22. Chameleon Collie
23. Bull Dog
24. Paw Pooch
25. Tusky Husky
26. Hot Dog
27. Tail Terrier
28. Mammoth Mutt
29. Prophetic Pup
30. Rex the Wonder Dog
31. Detective Chimp
32. Starlene
33. Mossy
34. Merle
35. Loafers
36. Storm
37. Topo
38. Ark
39. Fluffy
40. Betty
41. Geoffrey
42. B'dg
43. Sen-Tag
44. Fendor
45. Stripezoid
46. Zallion
47. Ribitz
48. Bzzd
49. Gratch
50. Buzzoo
51. Fossfur
52. Zhoomp
53. Eeny

KNOW YOUR VILLAIN PETS!

. Bizarro Krypto
. Ignatius
. Brainicat
. Mechanikat
.Dogwood
. General Manx
. Nizz
. Fer-El
. Crackers
0. Giggles
1. Artie Puffin
2. Griff
3. Waddles
4. Rozz
5. Mad Catter
6. Croward
7. Chauncey
8. Bit-Bit & X-43
9. Dr. Spider
0. Anna Conda
1. Mr. Mind
2. Sobek
3. Patches
4. Dex-Starr
5. Glomulus
6. Titano
7. Purring Pete
8. Kid Kitty
9. Scratchy Tom
0. Gat-Cat
1. Starro
2. Mama Ripples
3. Faye Precious
4. Limpy
5. Offie Lee
6. Misty
7. Sneezers
8. Johnny
9. Joey
0. Frankie
1. George
2. Whoosh
3. Pronto
4. Snorrt
5. Rolf
6. Squealer
7. Kajunn
8. Tootz
9. Eezix
0. Donald
1. Waxxee
2. Fimble
3. Webbik

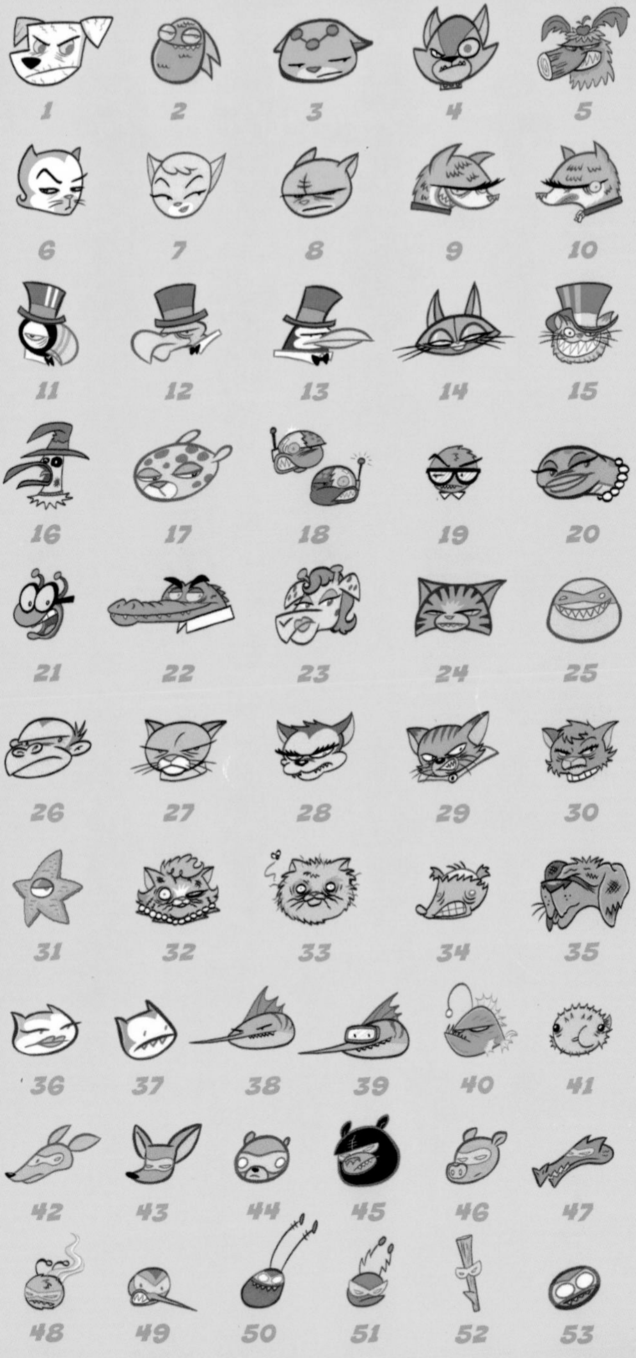
1 2 3 4 5
6 7 8 9 10
11 12 13 14 15
16 17 18 19 20
21 22 23 24 25
26 27 28 29 30
31 32 33 34 35
36 37 38 39 40 41
42 43 44 45 46 47
48 49 50 51 52 53

MEET THE AUTHOR!

John Sazaklis

John Sazaklis, a *New York Times* bestselling author, enjoys writing children's books about his favorite characters. To him, it's a dream come true. He has been reading comics and watching cartoons since before even the Internet! John lives with his beautiful wife in the Big Apple.

MEET THE ILLUSTRATOR!

Eisner Award-winner Art Baltazar

Art Baltazar is a cartoonist machine from the heart of Chicago! He defines cartoons and comics not only as an art style, but as a way of life. Currently, Art is the creative force behind *The New York Times* best-selling, Eisner Award-winning, DC Comics series Tiny Titans, and the co-writer for *Billy Batson and the Magic of SHAZAM!* Art is living the dream! He draws comics and never has to leave the house. He lives with his lovely wife, Rose, big boy Sonny, little boy Gordon, and little girl Audrey. Right on!

WORD POWER!

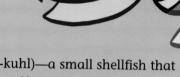

barnacle (BAR-nuh-kuhl)—a small shellfish that attaches itself to the sides of boats and rocks

beluga (buh-LOO-guh)—a toothed whale that becomes 10 to 15 feet long and white when adult

coral (KOR-uhl)—a colony of sea creatures, called polyps, together with its membranes and skeletons

porthole (PORT-hohl)—a small, round window in the side of a ship or a boat

throne (THROHN)—a fancy chair for a king or queen

toxic (TOK-sik)—poisonous, or dangerous to digest

trident (TRYE-dent)—a spear with three prongs

trinket (TRING-keht)—a thing of little value

ukulele (yoo-kuh-LAY-lee)—a small, four-stringed guitar originally made popular in Hawaii

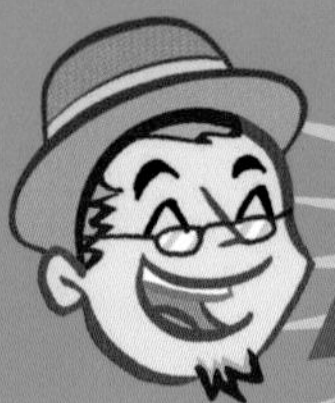

ART BALTAZAR SAYS:

AW YEAH!

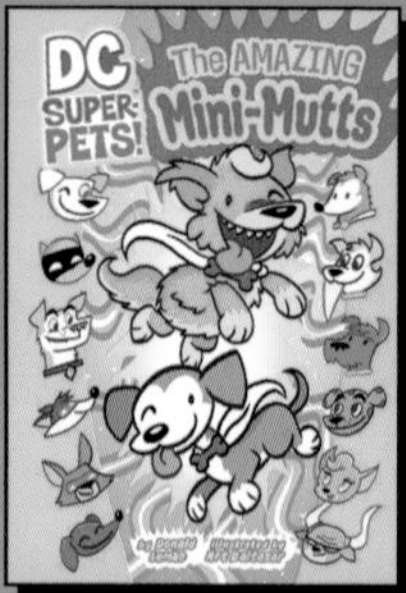
DC SUPER-PETS!
The AMAZING Mini-Mutts

HERO DOGS GALORE!

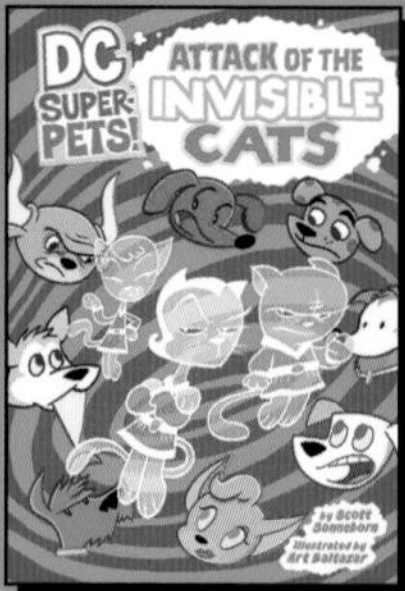
DC SUPER-PETS!
ATTACK OF THE INVISIBLE CATS

SPACE CANINE PATROL AGENCY!

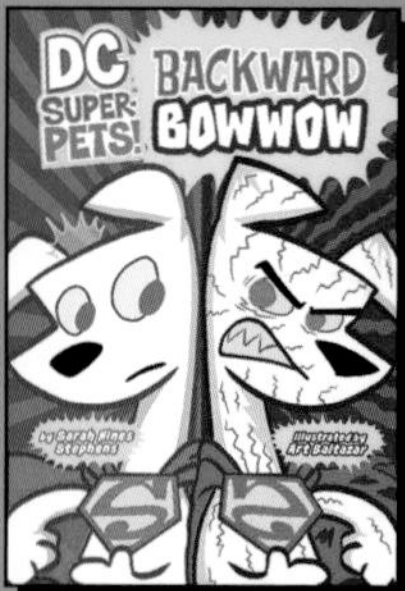
DC SUPER-PETS!
BACKWARD BOWWOW

KRYPTO THE SUPER-DOG!

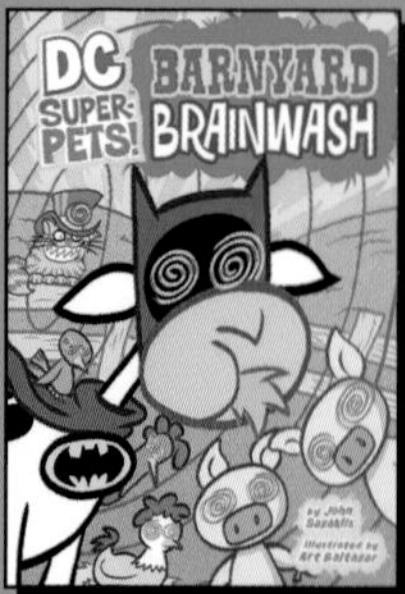
DC SUPER-PETS!
BARNYARD BRAINWASH

BATCOW!

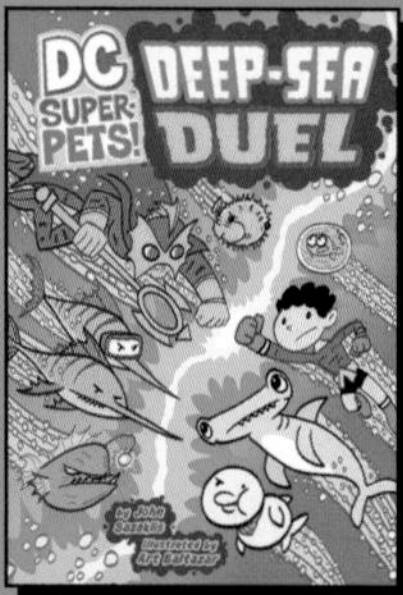
DC SUPER-PETS!
DEEP-SEA DUEL

FLUFFY AND THE AQUA-PETS!

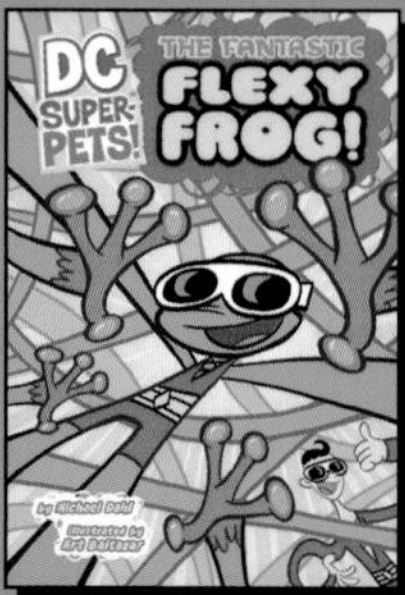
DC SUPER-PETS!
THE FANTASTIC FLEXY FROG!

PLASTIC FROG!

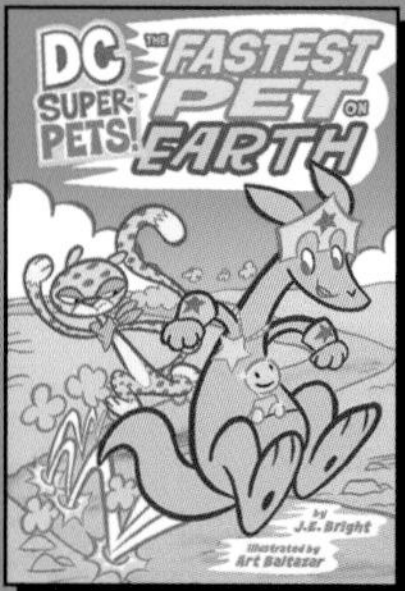
DC SUPER-PETS!
THE FASTEST PET ON EARTH

JUMPA THE KANGA!

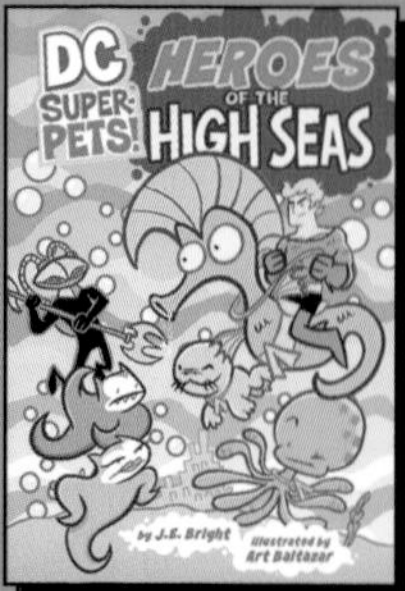
DC SUPER-PETS!
HEROES OF THE HIGH SEAS

STORM AND THE AQUA-PETS!

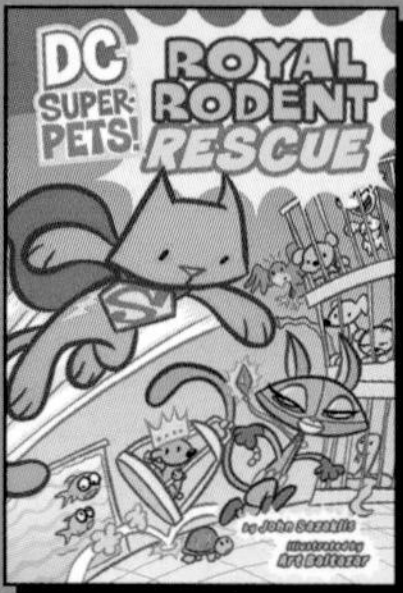
DC SUPER-PETS!
ROYAL RODENT RESCUE

STREAKY THE SUPER-CAT!

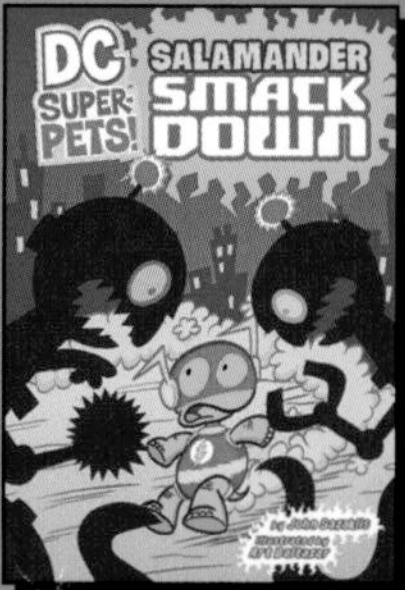
DC SUPER-PETS!
SALAMANDER SMACK DOWN

THE TERRIFIC WHATZIT!

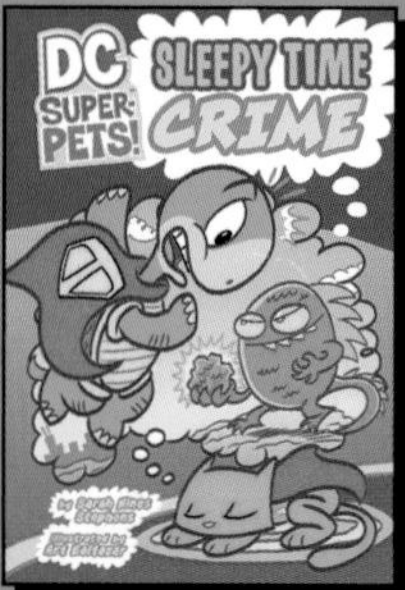
DC SUPER-PETS!
SLEEPY TIME CRIME

SUPER-TURTLE!

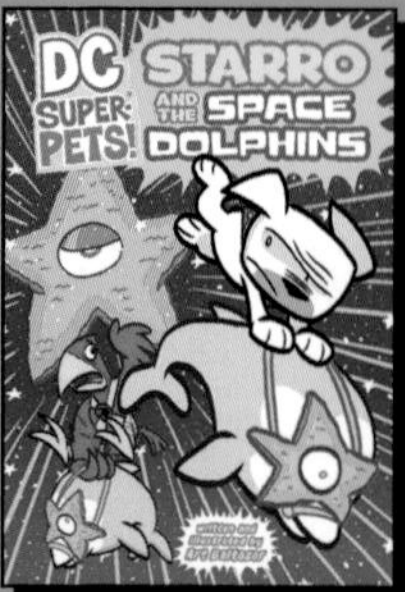
DC SUPER-PETS!
STARRO AND THE SPACE DOLPHINS

BIG TED AND DAWG!

Read all of these totally awesome stories today, starring all of your favorite DC SUPER-PETS!

GREEN LANTERN BUG CORPS!

SPOT!

ROBIN ROBIN AND ACE TEAM-UP!

SPACE CANINE PATROL AGENCY!

HOPPY!

BEPPO THE SUPER-MONKEY!

ACE THE BAT-HOUND!

KRYPTO AND ACE TEAM-UP!

B'DG, THE GREEN LANTERN!

THE LEGION OF SUPER-PETS!

COMET THE SUPER-HORSE!

DOWN HOME CRITTER GANG!

THE FUN DOESN'T STOP HERE!

Discover more:

- Videos & Contests!
- Games & Puzzles!
- Heroes & Villains!
- Authors & Illustrators!

@ www.capstonekids.com

Find cool websites and more books like this one
at www.facthound.com Just type in Book I.D.
9781404864894 and you're ready to go!

Picture Window Books

Published in 2013
A Capstone Imprint
1710 Roe Crest Drive
North Mankato, MN 56003
www.capstonepub.com

STAR26099

Cataloging-in-Publication Data is available
at the Library of Congress website.
ISBN: 978-1-4048-6489-4 (library binding)
ISBN: 978-1-4048-7662-0 (paperback)

Summary: Aquaman has invited his entire
family to his underwater kingdom — except
his evil half-brother, Ocean Master. But this
villain and his horrible hench-fish can't be
kept at bay. When they crash the reunion,
Aqualad and his Super-Pet, Fluffy, must put
the splashdown on these fishy foes!

Art Director & Designer: Bob Lentz
Editor: Donald Lemke
Creative Director: Heather Kindseth
Editorial Director: Michael Dahl

Printed in the United States of America
in North Mankato, Minnesota.
042016   009742R